Nobody's Perfect!

"Oh, Mom, Dad! Baby is miserable and all because I expected him to be the perfect pet for the mascot contest!" Missy told her parents. "Do you think he'll ever forgive me?"

Mr. Fremont put his hand on Missy's shoulder. "Only Baby can answer that question, honey."

Missy slowly and carefully joined Baby behind the sofa. He was shaking when Missy threw her arms around his neck.

Baby looked up at her. After a few seconds, he barked softly and began licking her face.

Missy laughed with relief—he *did* forgive her, after all!

THE MASCOT MESS

by Molly Albright

illustrated by Eulala Conner

Troll Associates

Library of Congress Cataloging-in-Publication Data

Albright, Molly.
    The mascot mess / by Molly Albright; illustrated by Eulala
Conner.
      p.   cm.
    Summary: Missy and her classmates scramble to turn their pets into
the best candidate for the soccer team mascot.
    ISBN 0-8167-1484-3 (lib. bdg.)   ISBN 0-8167-1485-1 (pbk.)
    [1. Schools—Fiction. 2. Pets—Fiction.] I. Conner, Eulala,
ill. II. Title.
PZ7.A325Mas 1989
[E]—dc19   88-15879

A TROLL BOOK, published by Troll Associates,
Mahwah, NJ 07430

Printed in the United States of America.

10 9 8 7 6 5 4 3 2 1

THE MASCOT MESS

CHAPTER

1

Melissa Fremont stared at the brightly colored ice cream menu on the wall, trying to decide if she was in a chocolate or a pistachio mood. Not far from the menu was another sign which read: NO BARE FEET OR DOGS ALLOWED! Missy sighed and shook her head. Bare feet she could understand—but no dogs? The way her Old English sheepdog Baby loved ice cream, he could easily be The Big Scoop's best customer!

The Big Scoop was the most popular ice cream parlor in Indianapolis. Not only were the sundaes delicious, but the waiters and waitresses dressed just like old-fashioned newspaper reporters, their order pads tucked into wide hatbands. It was also the perfect place for the Hills Point varsity soccer team to celebrate their second victory in a row!

"What's the scoop?" asked Betty, their waitress. Missy recognized Betty as one of the neighborhood high school girls. Betty pretended not to recognize Missy and her friends.

"I'll have a Front Page Special with pistachio ice cream please," Missy ordered, her mouth watering. A pistachio mood without a doubt!

"Hmmm," thought Willie out loud. Willie's real name was Wilhelmina Wagnalls, a name which was almost as long as her legs. "I guess I'll have a Hot Fudge Headline with nuts."

Betty glanced over her order pad and looked at Stephanie Cook. Stephanie flipped her long blond hair over her shoulders. "Just a small dish of vanilla ice cream for me."

Missy stared at Stephanie. "That's all you're having? At The Big Scoop? How come?"

"Because I would die if I accidentally dripped fudge sauce on my brand-new designer sweat suit, that's why! Besides," Stephanie added, turning to Emily Green, "I wouldn't want to get fat and gross! . . . What are you having, Emily?"

Emily's chubby face turned a bright red as she stared down at the table. "I'll just have a diet soda with ice."

Betty finished writing up the orders and was just about to walk away, when Emily called out, "Oh, and could you throw in a small scoop of Rocky Road?" Emily shrugged her shoulders. "Ice cream is loaded with calcium. I've got to have strong bones if I'm going to play on a winning team."

Missy smiled at Emily and raised her water glass. "To the best school soccer team in the whole U.S.A.! May we always reach our goals!"

"Hear, hear!" chanted Willie and Emily.

"Winning isn't everything, you know," said Stephanie impatiently.

"We know that!" Missy smiled, placing her water glass down with a clink. "Coach Harris is always reminding us that it's how we play the game that counts!"

"I wasn't thinking about that either, silly!" snapped Stephanie. "Willie—will you watch where you put your knees? They keep knocking into mine!"

"Can I help it if I have long legs?" Willie snapped back.

"What were you thinking of, Stephanie?" asked Emily, hoping to change the subject.

"If you must know, I was thinking of our team's image. Every winning team should have a mascot! Today at the game we didn't have one, and I was *so* embarrassed!"

Missy wrinkled her nose. "What exactly is a mascot?"

Stephanie rolled her eyes. "Didn't you notice a boy dressed in a chicken suit at the game today? That was the other team's mascot—they brought him along for good luck!"

"Well, he couldn't have been doing his job!" Emily laughed. "His team lost by ten points!"

Willie chuckled mischievously. "Sounds like a case of *fowl* play to me!"

Missy and Emily rolled in their seats with laughter. "Seems like the chicken was more *cluck* than luck!" howled Missy, holding her stomach. By now Betty was placing their orders in front of them on the table.

"I hope our waitress didn't hear those jokes," whispered Stephanie after Betty left for the next booth. "They were *soooooo* stupid!"

Missy was almost used to Stephanie's snooty remarks. Nevertheless, she did think the idea of having a mascot was a pretty good one—even if it did come from the head of Ms. Perfect!

"I think we should have a mascot too," Missy admitted, licking the gooey marshmallow topping from her spoon.

"Yeah," agreed Willie as she scraped hot fudge sauce from the side of her dish. "And I can think of a few boys at school I'd like to see in a chicken suit!"

"Our mascot doesn't have to be a boy in a chicken suit! It can be a real live animal!" suggested Stephanie.

Missy's eyes lit up with excitement. A real live animal just like her best friend Baby! Now Missy really liked Stephanie's idea. If Baby couldn't play on the soccer team, then at least he could be its mascot!

"Attention! Attention!" announced Missy dramatically. "Our search for a mascot has just come to an end. I hereby appoint my dog, Baby."

Stephanie pretended to choke on her ice cream. "Baby? That clumsy, hairy beast? No way! What would they call us? The Hills Point Babies?"

Missy hated when Stephanie made fun of her dog, especially his name. "His name happens to be Baby because he was just a tiny ball of fluff when I adopted him!" Missy and Baby were two of a kind—both adopted by the Fremont family.

Stephanie ignored Missy as a dreamy look came over her face. "If our mascot is to represent us and our team, then it has to be simple, yet elegant. Sleek, yet swift . . . "

"Are you thinking about an animal or a sports car?" demanded Missy.

"Well, I certainly wasn't thinking about a sheepdog!" shouted Stephanie. "Sheepdogs are klutzy—just like you, Missy Fremont!"

"Better klutzy than snobby like you, Stephanie Cook!" Missy shouted back.

Willie quickly leaned over the table so that she was halfway out of the seat. "Meowww! Woof, woof!" she cried. "Meowww! Woof, woof!"

"And what is that supposed to mean?" snapped Stephanie.

"It means that you two are fighting like cats and dogs!" exclaimed Willie. "Meowww! Woof!"

Missy laughed, but Stephanie was furious.

"Will you please stop it, Willie? People are beginning to stare!" Stephanie hissed. "And I do not like being called a cat *or* a dog. Now . . . about our mascot."

"I know," said Emily, slurping the last drop of her ice cream soda. "A lot of kids at school have pets. Why don't we have a contest for the best mascot? We can even ask Coach Harris and Ms. Van Sickel to be the judges."

Willie and Missy thought it was a terrific idea, but Stephanie snorted with disgust. "A contest? Oh, come on. Can't you be more original than that?"

Everyone sat quietly as Emily hung her head. All of a sudden Stephanie jumped up, snapping her fingers. "I have the best idea! Why don't we ask the kids at school to bring in their pets? Then Coach Harris and Ms. Van Sickel can decide which one would make the best mascot!"

"Hey!" cried Emily. "That's exactly what I said!" Missy and Willie gave Emily a weary look as if to say, "Forget it." Stephanie always had to be the one with the great idea—no matter whose it was!

"Well, what do you think?" Stephanie wanted to know. The others nodded their heads. In Missy's mind she could already see Baby being carried across the soccer field, the team singing "For He's a Jolly Good Fellow" at the top of their lungs. Baby had to win the mascot contest —he just had to!

"Good." Stephanie smiled slyly. "Then may the best pet win."

"I wish my parents would let me have a pet," sighed Emily. "Then I could enter it in the mascot contest."

"Why can't you have a pet, Emily?" asked Missy.

"My older sister Nancy is allergic to fur and feathers," said Emily. "You should hear her sneeze whenever she passes a zoo or a ski shop."

"A ski shop?" cried Stephanie.

"Down jackets," explained Emily. "You know, duck feathers."

Missy whistled through her teeth. "That bad, huh?" Then she glanced down at her purple wristwatch. "Uh-oh. I've got to head home now."

"Already?" asked Willie, disappointed.

"I . . . uh . . . have a chore to do," Missy lied.

"A chore," sighed Stephanie. "What a drag."

Missy couldn't bring herself to explain the real reason she was leaving. "If Stephanie finds out I want to rush home to watch *The Professor Pesty Show* on TV, I'll never hear the end of it!" thought Missy, staring at a smudge on the table. Stephanie watched only sappy soap operas like *How the Heart Throbs.*

Missy's thoughts were suddenly interrupted by a loud painful scream. "Owwww, Willie! You just stepped on my toe!" yelped Stephanie. "Will you get those daddy-long-legs out of my way once and for all?"

"All right already, Stephanie!" shouted an insulted Willie. She flung her legs out from under the table just as Betty was sauntering by with a tall root-beer float in her hand. Betty's high-heeled shoe suddenly hooked around Willie's ankle, sending her flying down the aisle. The foamy root beer went flying too—out of the glass and all over Stephanie.

Missy, Emily, and Willie gawked as the ice cream soda dripped down Stephanie's brand-new designer sweat suit!

"Ughhhhh!" she screamed. "My sweat suit is ruined! Ruined! I knew we shouldn't have come to a stupid ice cream parlor. I just knew it!"

Missy watched Stephanie sputtering like an angry wet hen, a scoop of strawberry ice cream sitting on her shoulder.

"I wonder what could be funnier," she giggled to herself. "*The Professor Pesty Show* . . . or Stephanie à la mode?"

2

Missy wasn't the only one who loved Professor Pesty. Baby loved him too. He especially liked Clarence the Wonder Dog, a Dalmatian who performed tricks. At times Clarence seemed even smarter than Professor Pesty himself!

That afternoon Pesty and Clarence were in tuxedos, giving a concert. Pesty was sawing away at a cello while Clarence banged on a piano with his paws. Baby barked happily at the television set, and Missy laughed so hard her stomach ached.

"Can I join the fun?" asked Mr. Fremont as he came into the living room.

"Oh, hi, Dad!" Missy gasped, exhausted from laughing. "We didn't disturb your practice, did we?" Missy's dad played first viola for the Indianapolis Symphony and usually practiced in the late afternoon.

Mr. Fremont shook his head and smiled at the TV screen. "I see I have some competition there," he said, watching the two aspiring musicians. "You and Baby really like that show, don't you?"

"We love it, Dad. Professor Pesty is the funniest man in the world!"

Mr. Fremont pretended to look hurt. "I thought I was!"

"Your jokes are cute, but Professor Pesty's jokes are hilarious!" Missy tried to explain. "Besides, a pie in the face just wouldn't be you!"

"Well, thank goodness for that!" Mr. Fremont laughed.

Professor Pesty and Clarence had finished the concert and were now taking their bows on television. Somebody tossed a bouquet of roses to Professor Pesty, but Clarence intercepted. He caught the flowers between his teeth as the studio audience applauded.

"Clarence," said Professor Pesty to the Wonder Dog. "I do believe we are ready for the Indianapolis Symphony!"

Missy spun around to stare at her father. "Dad, did you hear—"

"Well, how do you like that?" asked Mr. Fremont with a grin. "Nobody ever throws *me* roses after I've finished a concert!"

Just then they heard Mrs. Fremont opening the front door as she came home from work. Missy's mom was a kindergarten teacher. She usually came home wearing streaks of paint on Finger Paint Day and clay in her hair on Clay Day.

"I'm home!" she called. "Missy, one of your friends is here to see you."

Missy couldn't figure out who it could be. She had just seen most of her friends at The Big Scoop.

"It's Stephanie Cook!" added her mother.

"Stephanie!" gasped Missy. "Oh, no!"

She couldn't let Stephanie catch her watching *The Professor Pesty Show*. Mr. Fremont watched curiously as Missy dashed to the television to snap it off—just in time for Stephanie to enter the living room.

"Good afternoon, Mr. Fremont." Stephanie smiled sweetly. "It's so nice to see you again."

"Hi, Stephanie," answered Mr. Fremont. "You know, you came just in time to watch—"

"To watch Baby drink his water!" Missy interrupted, pushing Baby's water dish over to him.

"Thrills," said Stephanie sarcastically.

Mr. Fremont shrugged his shoulders and excused himself to greet Mrs. Fremont, who was still on the doorstep pouring sand out of her shoes from Sandbox Day.

When the two girls were alone in the living room, Missy looked at Stephanie from head to toe. To her surprise Ms. Perfect looked as cool as a cucumber, totally recovered from The Big Scoop disaster. She was wearing a pair of French jeans and a hand-painted T-shirt.

"What's up?" asked Missy, flopping into a chair.

"I just thought you'd want to hear the good news," answered Stephanie, strolling around the living room examining the knickknacks.

"Don't tell me," said Missy, pretending to guess. "Your mother is buying you a new designer sweat suit."

"Well, that too . . . but this news concerns the whole Hills Point soccer team," Stephanie told Missy, her eyes shining. "I just called Ms. Van Sickel and Coach Harris, and they both said my idea for a mascot contest is great!"

"You mean Emily's idea," Missy thought angrily.

"In fact," continued Stephanie, "Ms. Van Sickel said she'd announce the rules for the contest after soccer practice on Saturday morning!"

Missy thought the news was terrific, but something was keeping her from getting excited.

"I thought you of all people would be thrilled!" complained Stephanie.

"I am," Missy insisted. "Um . . . Stephanie?"

"Yes?"

"Do you . . . have an animal in mind . . . for the mascot?"

"Oh, Missy," sighed Stephanie. "Isn't it enough that I'm masterminding this whole contest? Who has time to think about animals?"

What a relief! The last thing Missy wanted to do was compete against Stephanie Cook—especially in a contest which involved Baby!

Stephanie walked around Baby. She watched him as he lapped at his water. "I suppose you'll be entering your . . . sheepdog."

Missy happily jumped from the chair. "You bet! Whatever the contest rules are, I'm sure Baby will win with flying colors!"

"I'm sure he will," muttered Stephanie, putting down the glass unicorn she was handling. "Oh, before I forget, do you ever watch *The Professor Pesty Show?*"

Missy stared at Stephanie. She couldn't have seen her watching the show—she just couldn't have! Missy gulped, nervously glancing down at her feet. "Professor who? Oh, you mean the guy on the kiddie show? I don't watch kiddie shows anymore. I watch *How the Heart Throbs.*"

"Too bad," said Stephanie. "Because my aunt Constance is the producer of *The Professor Pesty Show.* She invited me and a friend to a special Saturday afternoon taping. I was going to ask you if you'd like to go, but if you say you—"

"*The Professor Pesty Show?*" squealed Missy. "That's the funniest TV show in the whole world!"

"Then I guess you'd like to go," said Stephanie.

"Would I? Even Baby is crazy about Clarence the Wonder Dog, aren't you, Baby?" Baby panted and wagged his tail.

"Melissa Fremont!" shouted Stephanie. "If that dog comes within a mile of the television studio, I'll—"

"Okay, okay. It'll be just you and me," Missy promised. "Thanks for the offer, Stephanie."

Just then Mr. and Mrs. Fremont came into the living room with a big bowl of popcorn.

"Mom, Dad! Guess what?" cried Missy as her parents sat down on the sofa.

"You're going to outer space to start a Martian soccer team!" her father joked.

"Dad, be serious. Stephanie is taking me to see *The Professor Pesty Show* in a real TV studio!" Missy said excitely.

"Why, that's very nice of you, Stephanie," Mrs. Fremont said with surprise.

"Oh, I always try to do nice things for my friends," chirped Stephanie. Missy threw Stephanie a surprised look. "You've got to be kidding!" she thought.

"Would you like some popcorn, Stephanie?" Mr. Fremont asked.

"Oh, no, Mr. Fremont." Stephanie shook her head. "I wouldn't want to spoil my appetite for dinner." She said good-by to Missy's parents and headed for the door.

As Missy watched Stephanie cross the street, she couldn't help wondering. Why was Stephanie being so nice? It wasn't like her at all—especially after what had happened at The Big Scoop. Oh, well. Some things were just too hard to try to figure out.

Missy rejoined her parents in the living room. She sat down next to Baby on the floor and began scratching him behind his ears.

"Mom? Dad?" she asked. "Did you ever wish that you had adopted a perfect kid like Stephanie Cook instead of me?"

Mr. and Mrs. Fremont stared at Missy in surprise. Then Mrs. Fremont burst out laughing. Mr. Fremont shook his head.

"Missy, to us you *are* the perfect kid, and we love you exactly as you are!" exclaimed Mr. Fremont.

"You know, honey, kids like Stephanie who try all the time to be 'perfect' are not necessarily perfectly happy," explained Mrs. Fremont.

Missy thought about what her parents had said. "Does that mean I can stay a klutz?" she asked as she squeezed between them on the sofa.

"Just promise me one thing, Melissa Fremont," said Missy's father as he tried to tickle her.

"What?" asked Missy.

"That you'll always stay exactly the way you are!"

"Okay! Okay! I promise!" Missy laughed. She had to be the most ticklish person in the world.

Suddenly Baby barked and leapt up onto the sofa, practically knocking the popcorn out of Mrs. Fremont's hands. He flopped down so that his front half was draped over Missy's and Mr. Fremont's legs.

"Hey," said Missy. "I'll bet *The Professor Pesty Show* is still on." She ran to turn on the television, just in time for everyone to see Clarence the Wonder Dog on a pair of roller skates. Baby snorted and wagged his tail in Mrs. Fremont's face.

"I can't believe I'm going to an actual taping of my favorite show," said Missy as the Fremonts all laughed and munched popcorn. "I'm so excited!"

In fact, she thought, the only thing that could possibly be more exciting would be seeing Baby become mascot of the Hills Point varsity soccer team!

CHAPTER

3

"**W**ait up!" Missy called as she and Baby ran to catch up with Stephanie, Willie, and Emily. They usually took the path along Hills Point Pond on their way to the soccer field on Saturdays. The pond was separated from the path by a row of bushes, but they could still feel the cool breeze from the water.

When Stephanie caught sight of Baby, she furiously threw down her soccer ball.

"And what is *he* doing here?" she demanded, pointing to Baby.

"I've decided to bring Baby to soccer practice today for the announcement of the mascot contest."

Stephanie glared at Missy. "Very sneaky, Melissa Fremont. Getting your dog to butter up the judges before the contest is even announced!"

"I simply brought Baby so he could hear the contest rules for himself," insisted Missy. "Besides, you said yourself that you didn't have a mascot in mind."

Stephanie's gaze quickly darted away from Missy's.

"Well, do you, Stephanie?" asked Missy. "Do you have a mascot in mind?"

"I told you I didn't, didn't I?" she snapped.

Willie waved her arms impatiently. "Can we please stop arguing and go to soccer practice already? Gee whiz!"

"Come on, Baby. Let's go," Missy told her dog. "You're going to love seeing us practice."

A moment of silence passed before Stephanie gave Missy a sly look. "Oh, I agree. Baby is going to *love* soccer practice . . . just like Willie or Emily will *love* seeing *The Professor Pesty Show*!"

Missy froze. There was no way she was going to miss a taping of *The Professor Pesty Show*.

"Go back home, Baby," she said.

Baby looked at Missy with a confused whine. His ears flattened against his head and his tail dropped between his legs. There was no mistaking it—Baby was insulted and Missy felt awful.

"Oh, Baby," pleaded Missy. "Try to understand!"

Stephanie watched with a victorious grin as Missy struggled to turn the big sheepdog around.

Finally, Baby slowly turned and began trudging up the path toward home. Missy reluctantly joined her friends as they continued on their way to soccer practice. They didn't get very far, for just a few moments later they heard a frantic barking sound.

"That's Baby!" Missy cried. She'd know her dog's bark anywhere.

"It sounds like it's coming from the pond!" cried Willie.

"Oh, no!" gasped Missy. "I hope Baby didn't fall in!"

Stephanie muttered with disgust as they tore through the long row of bushes.

"There he is!" shouted Missy. Sure enough, there was Baby standing on the edge of the pond, barking at the water. Soon everyone saw just what he was barking at—a scrawny, dirty gray cat floating on a rubber tire! The cat was yowling desperately as it tried to cling to the slippery tire.

Quickly, Missy and Willie picked up a long branch that was lying on the ground. Together they tried to reach the tire with the branch, but it didn't work. It wasn't long enough.

"Why don't you stick your leg out, Willie?" cracked Stephanie.

"Very funny, Stephanie Cook!" Willie panted.

Emily chewed her nails as she nervously watched the rescue attempt. Stephanie appeared bored as she picked up her soccer ball. "Here. This will make it budge," she sighed, ready to throw the ball at the tire.

"Stephanie—don't!" screamed Missy. "You'll knock the cat into the water!"

Emily began to wail. "What will we do? We can't just leave the poor thing out there!"

At that moment Baby leapt into the pond with a huge splash. The four girls watched with amazement as the sheepdog began swimming toward the tire and the cat.

"Yayyyyyy!" shouted Missy happily. "Baby to the rescue!"

Baby reached the tire, and with his nose pushed it safely back to shore. Emily was the first to reach for the cat. Taking its shaking body in her arms, she cooed softly. "You're safe now . . . you're safe."

"Thanks to Baby!" Missy said proudly, giving her dog a big hug. Baby gave his wet body a shake, spraying the girls with a shower of pond water.

"Oh, great!" groaned Stephanie as everyone else laughed. "Now we're late, soaking wet, and we smell like a fish pond too!"

The girls ignored Stephanie as they tended to the trembling cat.

"What should we do with him?" Missy asked.

"Do with him?" cried Stephanie. "Leave him here! He's a gross flea bag. We have no idea where he's been!"

Willie rolled her eyes at Stephanie. "You'd be a gross flea bag too, if you were drifting on a tire for hours! Or days!"

The argument was interrupted when Emily suddenly announced, "I'm taking him home!"

Everyone turned to Emily as she dried him off with her sweater. "I always wanted a pet and now I'm finally going to have one!"

"But, Emily," said Missy. "You're not allowed to have a pet. You told us so yourself."

"Yeah, and what about your allergic sister?" Stephanie reminded Emily. "Don't tell me you forgot about her!"

"Nancy is away at college." Emily shrugged. "Besides, when my mom and dad see Sebastian, they'll fall in love with him for sure!"

Missy, Willie, and Stephanie wrinkled their noses. "Sebastian?" they cried together.

"I'm naming him after a beautiful tiger I saw at the circus last year," explained Emily. "Can't you see his stripes?"

"Under all that filth?" snorted Stephanie with disgust. "I'm surprised you can even see he's a cat!"

Emily was not about to be talked out of taking Sebastian home. She even decided to miss soccer practice that day.

"I'll drop Baby off at your house on my way home, Missy," Emily offered as she wrapped Sebastian in her sweater.

Emily waved back to her friends as she carefully walked off, Baby at her side and Sebastian in her arms.

"Bye, Emily!" called Missy.

"See you, Em!" called Willie.

"Good luck, Emily!" called Stephanie sweetly. "You're going to *neeeeed* it!"

Missy and Willie shot Stephanie a look of warning as they finally continued on their way to the soccer field.

"Nice practice today, team," Coach Harris told the Hills Point varsity soccer team as they collapsed on the grass in an exhausted heap. After everyone caught their breath, Ms. Van Sickel approached the team, holding a clipboard.

"This is it! This is it!" Missy nudged Willie and Stephanie.

Ms. Van Sickel cleared her throat a couple of times as she waited for the team to quiet down. Ms. Van Sickel never stopped being a teacher— even on Saturdays.

"As I promised," she began, "here are the rules for the Hills Point Varsity Soccer Team Mascot Contest. It will be held one week from today, after our game with the Crestview Waves." Ms. Van Sickel went on to explain that the contest would be open to all Hills Point School students and their pets. "The winner will be judged on these four categories," continued Ms. Van Sickel, peering down at her clipboard. "Number one . . . beauty and charm. Number two . . talent. Number three . . . intelligence. And number four . . . school spirit! Good luck to all, and may the best pet win!"

The announcement was followed by a rousing team cheer as everyone collected copies of the rules to hand out at school. As they scrambled to leave, Willie asked Missy if she thought Baby still had a good chance.

"A good chance?" Missy cried. "Baby is the most talented, beautiful, charming, intelligent and spirited dog in Indianapolis!"

"We'll see about that," snickered Stephanie.

But just as Missy was about to ask Stephanie what she meant, they saw Emily walking toward the field. She was carrying Sebastian and trudging slowly.

"Hey, Em!" called Willie. "What was the ver-

dict?" Emily hung her head. As she came nearer, Missy could see tears in her eyes.

"Emily?" asked Missy softly. "Did your parents say you couldn't keep the cat?"

Emily nodded, choking back a sob. "Nancy is coming home from college next week. That's how long I have to keep Sebastian!"

"Ha! I knew it!" Stephanie smiled meanly.

Missy put her arm around Emily. "Oh, well. Just think. You'll have one whole week to have fun with Sebastian!"

"And I'll help you find a good home for him," Willie volunteered. "I know practically every family in Hills Point."

Missy wanted to stick around to cheer Emily up, but Stephanie was tugging at her sleeve.

"Missy, I can't believe you forgot," she said.

"Forgot what?" asked Missy.

"*The Professor Pesty Show!*" cried Stephanie. "We have to be at the studio in two hours, remember?"

How could Missy forget? She had to hurry home to change into her favorite outfit. After all, she was soon going to meet two of the biggest stars on television!

"Don't you think I'm lucky to have a real TV producer for an aunt?" Stephanie asked Missy, forgetting that Missy's aunt Jessica wrote jingles for TV commercials.

Missy nodded and smiled. "Sure," she thought. "But I'm the really lucky one—soon I'm going to have the Hills Point varsity soccer team mascot for a pet!"

"And now, girls," announced Stephanie's aunt Constance as she flung open the door leading to one of the dressing rooms, "I think you'll recognize this gentleman!"

The man sitting in the make-up chair had his back to the door, but in the reflection of the mirror, Missy saw that it was none other than Professor Pesty!

"Professor, this is my niece Stephanie Cook and her friend Melissa Fremont," Aunt Constance told him. "They came to see the show today."

Professor Pesty smiled as he stood up from the chair and walked over to Missy and Stephanie.

Missy stared up at Professor Pesty, not believing she was only inches away from the funniest man on television.

"Well, hi, Stephanie . . . Melissa. So glad you could make it to the show," Professor Pesty said cheerfully, holding his hand out first to Stephanie.

"Hello, Mr. Pesty," Stephanie said coolly. "It's been a while since I've seen your show, but I understand it's really big with the *little* kids."

Professor Pesty raised an eyebrow at Aunt Constance. Then he reached his hand over to Missy.

"Hi, Melissa!"

Missy opened her mouth to speak but nothing came out. She felt like she had swallowed a coconut!

"Say something," Stephanie hissed, giving her a nudge.

"P-P-Professor Pesty! I love your show!" Missy's words came tumbling out.

"Oh, no," thought Missy as they shook hands. "That was a dumb thing to say. He probably hears that all the time."

But Professor Pesty acted as friendly as ever. "Girls, I'm not quite finished with my make-up, so how would you like someone to give you a tour of the studio?"

"I was just about to suggest that myself," said Aunt Constance with a smile. Missy had decided that Aunt Constance was a nice person—too nice to be related to Stephanie.

"I thought I'd die when you couldn't even say hello to Professor Pesty," groaned Stephanie as they left the dressing room. Missy ignored Stephanie as she turned to ask Aunt Constance if they were going to be meeting Clarence the Wonder Dog.

"Oh, yes!" answered Aunt Constance, nodding toward the next dressing room. "He usually rests before the show, but you'll get to meet him between takes."

At that moment a man carrying a water dish came down the hall and went into the room. Judging by the gold star on the water dish, Missy decided it belonged to Clarence.

"Excuse me, Richard," said Aunt Constance just as he was about to open the door to the dressing room. "But what kind of water is that?"

"This? This is ice cold . . . tap water," the man said nervously.

"Tap water?" Aunt Constance gasped as she leaned against the door. "That will not do, Richard! You know that Clarence drinks only *sparkling spring water!*"

"I'll run out to get some right now!" promised the man as he hurried back up the hall.

Aunt Constance turned to Missy and Stephanie. "Stars can be very demanding, you know."

Missy looked over at Stephanie, who was nodding as if she knew exactly what Aunt Constance meant.

"Not Baby," thought Missy. "He's going to be the nicest star there ever was. Even Stephanie will love him!"

The tour of the television studio was very exciting. Missy recognized the set of *The Professor Pesty Show* right away. There were huge television cameras everywhere and microphones hanging from the ceiling. A camera operator named Roberta let Stephanie and Missy look through the camera lens. After that Aunt Constance took them into the control room, where the director explained how some of the equipment worked. Missy had the most fun when they visited the wardrobe room to try on some of Professor Pesty's bow ties and hats. But when everyone in the studio began hustling to their places on the set, Missy knew that *The Professor Pesty Show* was about to begin!

"Missy," hissed Stephanie. "This is not your living room, you know!"

"I—I can't help it," whispered Missy, trying to muffle her laughter with her hand. "He's so funny!"

The show they were there to see was one of the funniest Missy had ever seen. Professor Pesty and Clarence were dressed in oversized chef hats. They were trying to cook a gourmet dog food dish from the famous canine cooking school in Paris, The Sor-bone. Professor Pesty wore a red and white apron which read THE FOOD HERE IS FOR THE DOGS and Clarence was standing over a huge bowl with an electric mixer buzzing away between his teeth.

"Zee recipeee calls for . . . one bedroom sleeper!" Professor Pesty announced with a phony French accent. Missy thought she'd split her sides when Professor Pesty tossed a chewed-up slipper into the bowl.

"And now . . . scent of mailman!" he called out next, holding up a perfume bottle. Professor Pesty took the lid off the bottle and dumped the

entire contents into the bowl. This time Stephanie had to clap her hand over Missy's mouth to keep her from laughing out loud. If only Baby were here to join the fun, Missy kept thinking.

They watched as Professor Pesty slid the bowl into a fake oven. After a few seconds he opened the door. The bowl was gone and in its place was a bone on a silver platter!

"Cut!" shouted the director. "That was perfect!" The crew was told they would be taking a ten-minute break while Professor Pesty changed his costume.

"Well, how do you like the show so far?" Aunt Constance asked, putting her arms around Stephanie and Missy.

"Great!" cried Missy. "It's even funnier in real life than it is on TV!"

"Aunt Constance?" asked Stephanie. "Why does the set look so much bigger on television than it really is?"

"I thought you never watch the show, Stephanie," Missy said innocently. Stephanie shot Missy a look while Aunt Constance explained how a special camera lens can make things appear larger on the television screen.

All of a sudden they were interrupted by Clarence the Wonder Dog, who ran over to greet them.

"Hey, it's Clarence!" Missy cried happily. Clarence sat down and shook both Missy's and Stephanie's hands. Missy couldn't believe she was actually petting Clarence the Wonder Dog! She was also surprised to see that Clarence enjoyed having his ears scratched just like Baby did.

"He's such a friendly dog!" exclaimed Missy.

"Clarence is very good-natured. He loves people," explained Aunt Constance. "That's why I think he'd make a wonderful mascot for your soccer team."

Missy swallowed hard. "Mascot . . . for our soccer team?" She turned to look at Stephanie, who stood with a sly smile on her face.

"Uh-oh. I suppose Stephanie wanted it to be a surprise," Aunt Constance said. "But now that it's out . . . I'm letting Clarence enter your contest for team mascot. I think it would be wonderful publicity for the show, don't you?"

Just then the stage manager called Aunt Constance to check a problem with one of the props. When she was gone, Missy glared at Stephanie. "You'll do anything to keep Baby from becoming mascot, won't you?"

Stephanie just tossed a strand of her hair over her shoulder. "Oh, don't get so excited. Clarence will compete fairly in the contest just like your Baby."

Compete fairly? How could any of the pets compete fairly against Clarence the Wonder Dog? It wasn't fair at all!

"We'll call ourselves the Hills Point Wonders," Stephanie said, kneeling down to pat Clarence. "Won't that be neat?"

Missy was about to tell Stephanie what she thought of her dirty trick, when they were joined by Professor Pesty, wearing a silly wig and a polka-dotted bow tie.

"Say, girls," he said with a wide grin. "How would you both like to be on television?"

Missy's and Stephanie's mouths dropped open.

"Television?" Stephanie gushed. "I was always told I should be on the screen!"

"Yeah," mumbled Missy. "You and the flies."

Before they knew it, Missy and Stephanie were standing in front of the cameras. Stephanie was holding a box of Rinky Dink cereal and Missy, a tube of Grin toothpaste. From the corner of her eye Missy could see Stephanie pouting at the camera like a high-fashion model. All Missy could think about was how much she hated Stephanie for playing another one of her famous sneaky tricks! As her anger grew and grew, she could feel her fist clutching the tube of Grin toothpaste tighter and tighter. But Missy didn't realize the strength of her own grip—until the cap suddenly popped off, sending globs of toothpaste squirting straight at Stephanie Cook!

"Yecccchhhh!" screamed Stephanie as the toothpaste exploded out of the tube and oozed down her face. "Gross! Gross!"

"Cut!" yelled the director. Missy dropped the tube of toothpaste while Clarence began to bark and whine.

"Oh, dear!" gasped Aunt Constance as she ran over. "We'll have to cut that out, won't we?"

Missy was about to apologize, when Professor Pesty boomed, "Cut that out? Are you kidding? That was hilarious—a real killer!"

Stephanie stared at Professor Pesty, horrified. "What? You want to show that on television? You can't!"

"Sure we can," chuckled Professor Pesty. "The kids will love it!"

Stephanie turned to Aunt Constance, hoping she would come to her rescue, but she was already laughing along with Professor Pesty.

"Come to think of it, it was pretty funny, Stephanie!"

Wiping the toothpaste off her face with her sleeve, Stephanie turned to Missy.

"Melissa Fremont, how could you do this to me?"

As Stephanie huffed off the set, Missy turned to see Clarence rehearsing for the next scene. He was dancing on his hind legs to a popular hit song.

"How could she *do* this to me?" wailed Missy as she sadly watched Clarence the Wonder Dog dancing his way to fame. "How can Baby ever compete with Clarence the Wonder Dog?"

CHAPTER

5

By Tuesday afternoon everyone at Hills Point School was talking about the upcoming mascot contest. Rob Lopez was going to enter his "multi-talented" hamster, Hamlet. Candice Kramer felt that her garden snake, Icky, was a sure winner; Harvey Goodman, the school computer whiz, was already working on a pet robot.

"Missy!" called Willie as she and Emily ran to meet her in the school yard after school. "Is it true?"

"Is what true?" Missy asked as she tried to stuff her social studies book into her knapsack.

"Is Stephanie really entering Clarence the Wonder Dog in the mascot contest?"

Missy hated to be reminded, but she sighed and nodded her head.

Emily put her hand on Missy's shoulder. "That

must make you feel just awful, Missy. I know how much you wanted Baby to be mascot."

Missy swung her knapsack over her shoulder and smiled. "I have a whole week to turn Baby into a wonder dog."

"A wonder dog? Oh, come on, Missy!" groaned Willie. "What can you do with Baby in just one week? Training a dog takes months!"

"Are you saying that my dog needs that much work?" asked Missy, pretending to be insulted. "Actually, Baby has always been a wonder dog. He just needs some, you know, brush-up lessons."

As the three friends began leaving the school yard, Missy asked Emily how Sebastian was doing.

"He's fine," Emily said, forcing a smile.

"We're going to find him a great home this afternoon. Right, Em?" asked Willie enthusiastically.

"Sure," answered Emily sadly.

Missy decided when she got home that if she was to turn Baby into a wonder dog by Saturday, her plans would have to be organized very carefully. The first step was to list each competition for the mascot contest on a piece of paper.

"Okay, Baby," she told her dog. "You'll be rated for each competition on a scale of one to ten. This way I'll get to see where you need the most help."

Missy examined the first category, which was beauty and charm. "Hmmm. You've always been a charmer, Baby, but as for beauty"— she looked at Baby with his long, matted hair hanging over his eyes and his feet caked with mud—"a definite . . . three," she sighed, making a mark on her list.

The phone rang and Missy went to answer it. It was probably her mother or father. Mrs. Fremont had to work late that day and Mr. Fremont had to go to work early.

"Hello?" said Missy, her eyes still on her list.

"Missy? It's me. Stephanie."

Missy almost dropped the receiver when she heard the voice of Stephanie Cook. She was sure Stephanie wasn't speaking to her, especially after the toothpaste incident on *The Professor Pesty Show*. What could she want now?

"Hi, Stephanie. What's new?" Missy asked.

"I was just calling to see if you were watching *The Professor Pesty Show*," answered Stephanie. "Clarence the Wonder Dog *and* my contestant for the mascot contest is doing the most outrageous—"

"No, I wasn't watching it!" snapped Missy. "I was in the middle of doing something else."

"Oh? What?" asked Stephanie.

"Ummm . . . I was thinking of taking Baby for a haircut," Missy answered.

"Oh? Where?" Stephanie asked again.

Why was she asking so many questions? "Where he always goes," Missy answered, hesitating. "To The Canine Clipper."

Missy could hear Stephanie laughing on the other end of the line. "The Canine Clipper? No wonder Baby always looks like a scrub mop. Clarence goes to The Jet Set Pet!"

For the first time in her life Missy slammed

the receiver down. The Jet Set Pet was the chicest dog-grooming parlor in town, and it was very expensive. How could Stephanie expect Baby to go there?

But then again, Missy thought as she looked over at Baby, if he went to The Jet Set Pet, it might improve his chances. Wouldn't that show Stephanie?

Baby walked over to Missy and nuzzled his nose against her hand.

"Oh, well," Missy sighed. "This is a special occasion and I do have twenty dollars saved up. Maybe The Jet Set Pet is worth a shot."

Missy looked up The Jet Set Pet in the telephone directory. She dialed the number carefully. After about three rings a woman answered.

"Jet Set Pet. Good afternoon," she said.

"Good afternoon," Missy replied. "How much do you charge to trim a sheepdog?"

"Hungarian or English?" the woman wanted to know.

Missy wrinkled her nose. "English . . . *Old* English," she answered.

"An Old English sheepdog is sixty dollars for a wash, cut, and blow-dry," said the woman as though she were reading from a list.

"Sixty dollars?" cried Missy.

"We do have a special offer on Tuesdays," the woman told Missy. "If you let one of our stylists experiment on your dog, it's absolutely free."

"A free haircut at The Jet Set Pet!" Missy squealed. Immediately, she made a four-thirty appointment for Baby. She smiled at Baby as she hung up the phone. "Only the best for my best friend!"

The Jet Set Pet was nothing like The Canine Clipper. It was even fancier than most of the hair-cutting salons Missy's parents went to. Rock music blared throughout the shop while colorful lights flashed on and off. There were all sorts of exotic plants hanging from the ceiling and pictures of elegant dogs pinned to the walls. From the front desk, where Missy and Baby stood, they could see dogs of every breed lounging on high tables. They were surrounded by fashionably dressed stylists cutting and blow-drying their hair.

As she looked around, Missy caught sight of a young man with a pair of scissors. He wouldn't take his eyes off Baby for a second!

A woman dressed in a red leather suit checked Baby's name off a long list. The small sign on her desk told Missy that she was the manager.

"This is our first visit," said Missy cheerfully.

The manager looked up from her list and peered at Baby. "I can see that," she sniffed coldly.

Missy was certain that she had come face-to-face with a grown-up Stephanie, especially when the manager flipped her long blond hair over her shoulder and sighed.

"Your stylist will be Claudia," said the manager briskly.

"Fine with me," agreed Missy, not knowing one stylist from another. All of a sudden the young man with the scissors stomped over to the desk.

"I heard that, Sally!" he cried out angrily. "It just isn't fair! Claudia always gets the interesting dogs!"

"But, Lance, I have you scheduled for the Anderson beagle at four forty-five," explained the manager.

"Oh, no! Not another beagle, please!" wailed the young man. He pointed dramatically to Baby. "I want to work on *that* dog!"

Missy looked down at Baby and puffed her chest out proudly.

"Why that dog, Lance?" the manager wanted to know.

"Sally, this animal is the ultimate challenge! Look at all this hair, just look at it!" Lance insisted, running his hands through Baby's thick coat. "Why, I feel like a sculptor who has just come across the most incredible piece of rock!"

"Did you hear that, Baby?" whispered Missy. "You are going to be a work of art!"

Missy watched the two argue back and forth until Sally finally agreed to let Lance work on Baby.

"You don't know how long I've waited for a dog like this!" Lance cried as he took Baby's collar.

"Just give him a trim, please," Missy called as Lance excitedly led Baby behind a beaded curtain and into the back of the shop.

Missy couldn't see Baby getting his hair cut, so she decided to pass some time watching a French

poodle get a manicure. The little dog was actually having pink nail polish painted on all four paws!

"What a place," thought Missy. "No wonder Clarence the Wonder Dog comes here!"

After an hour passed, Missy became impatient. She took a chair near the curtain, where she waited for Baby.

Soon she was fantasizing about the mascot contest on Saturday. She imagined how all heads would turn when Baby appeared on the soccer field with his new Jet Set haircut.

"Such an elegant creature!" Ms. Van Sickel would gush.

"The look of a champion!" Coach Harris would gasp.

"Go chase a fire truck, Clarence!" Aunt Constance would say. "I have a new star now!"

But Missy's pleasant fantasy came to an end when the curtain finally opened and out stepped Lance with an unusual-looking dog. As Missy opened her mouth to ask Lance where Baby was, she realized that the dog *was* Baby!

"Well? Isn't it wild?" Lance asked Missy proudly.

Wild was not the word. Baby looked like the Sheepdog from Outer Space! His hair was sticking out in all directions as if he had seen a ghost. On top of his head was a wispy ponytail, while his own tail was crimped in such a way that it resembled a mass of party streamers. And if that wasn't enough, Baby's coat was streaked all over with lavender dye!

"What did you do to my dog?" shouted Missy

when she finally found her voice. "What did you do to my dog?"

Everyone at The Jet Set Pet turned to stare at Missy, including a pampered Pekingese who gave an annoyed yelp. Sally hurried over to see what the commotion was all about.

"Now, you did agree to let our stylist experiment on your dog," she said, trying to calm Missy down. "That is part of our special deal."

Missy could only gawk at Baby in disbelief.

"Mark my words. In two years, all sheepdogs will look like this," said Lance, stepping back to admire his work. "Just think of Baby as a . . . trend setter!"

While Missy walked her "trend setter" home, she wondered if The Jet Set Pet ever experimented on Clarence the Wonder Dog. "What could they do with a Dalmatian?" she thought. "Connect the dots?"

Missy hoped she and Baby wouldn't run into anyone on their way home, but they did run into Willie, Emily, and Sebastian the cat.

Willie and Emily stared at Baby.

"Boy," said Willie. "And I thought *we* were having a bad day."

Missy tried to ignore the comment. "Didn't you find a home for Sebastian?" she asked, patting the cat on its head.

"No, we did not!" Willie complained. "Emily is being totally impossible. She wasn't satisfied with one single family that wanted to adopt Sebastian."

"They just weren't good enough for Sebastian," insisted Emily, clutching the cat tightly to her chest.

"What was wrong with the Berkes?" Willie wanted to know.

"The Berkes?" cried Emily. "There were too many children in that home. Sebastian would go crazy!"

"Then what was wrong with Mr. and Mrs. Davis?" asked Willie.

"They had *no* children," explained Emily. "Sebastian would be bored stiff!"

Willie looked at Missy and threw her hands up in despair. "See what I mean?"

Missy could see Emily wasn't going to be satisfied with any home for Sebastian—unless that home was her own!

As the girls walked home, Missy could see people pointing and staring at Baby.

"What an unusual dog!" said one woman. "He must be from another country."

"Or another planet!" a man said, laughing.

Missy looked down at her lavender sheepdog and sighed. "Oh, well. We'll just have to work extra hard on the talent competition, that's all."

CHAPTER 6

"**C**ome on, Baby!" Missy pleaded, holding a Doggie Yum-Yum over his head. "Roll over!"

Baby looked up at the dog biscuit, yawned, and shut his eyes.

"Darn, darn, darn!" cried Missy, throwing aside the biscuit and falling down on the sofa.

"Having a rough day?" asked Mr. Fremont.

"Oh, Dad," Missy complained. "For two whole afternoons I've tried to teach Baby one easy trick and so far we've gotten nowhere."

Mr. Fremont blinked. "What about his jump-through-the-hoop-and-catch-the-Frisbee trick?" he asked.

"That one's no good, Dad. Everyone's seen him do it." Missy had taught Baby to do that trick for a class project, a videotape about her family.

"How long did it take you to teach Baby his trick for the tape?" Mr. Fremont wanted to know.

"About two weeks," Missy admitted. "But I have only a few days! What am I going to do?"

"Get some expert help." Mr. Fremont picked up a copy of the Yellow Pages and flipped to the letter A. " 'Skip Martin—Animal Trainer,' " Mr. Fremont began to read. " 'Who Says You Can't Teach an Old Dog New Tricks?' "

"That's fine, Dad," said Missy. "Except I can't even teach a new dog old tricks!" She crawled over to Baby and looked him straight in the eye. "Roll over, you," she said.

Missy groaned as Baby gave her a wet lick on the nose.

"Why don't you take a break and watch *The Professor Pesty Show*?" advised Mr. Fremont. "You look like you could use a laugh."

"Please, Dad!" Missy shivered. "The last thing I want to see now is Clarence the Wonder Dog!" She gave Baby a frustrated look. "I can't understand it. I've even tried rewarding him with a dog biscuit."

At that moment Mrs. Fremont came through the door carrying a cardboard box. "Hi. Home at last!"

"What's in the box, honey?" asked Mr. Fremont.

"I passed the bakery on my way home from work and I just couldn't resist," Mrs. Fremont replied, opening the box dramatically. "Ta-daaaaaaa! Chocolate fudge brownies!"

As soon as he heard the words "chocolate

brownies," Baby's ears perked up. Next thing everyone knew, Baby was actually rolling over!

"Mom! Dad! Look!" Missy shrieked happily. She ran over to grab a brownie from the box, and she held it over Baby's head. "Roll over," she commanded. Sure enough, Baby did roll over—not once, but twice! Missy broke off a tiny piece of the brownie and gave it to Baby, who ate it instantly. Maybe Baby wouldn't roll over for a dog biscuit, but he'd sure do it for a chocolate fudge brownie!

"Say, Mom?" Missy asked. "Did you see Stephanie Cook on her lawn when you came in?"

"As a matter of fact, I did," answered Mrs. Fremont.

"Great! Come on, Baby," she told her dog. "You are about to give your first performance."

With the soft grass below and a delicious brownie above, Baby was rolling over more than ever. From the corner of her eye Missy could see Stephanie watching from her lawn across the street.

"Bravo! Bravo!" Stephanie clapped, to Missy's surprise. "Is that the trick Baby is going to do for the mascot contest?"

"Yup!" Missy called back. "Pretty amazing, huh?"

Stephanie stretched lazily on her lawn chair. "I suppose it is, for an ordinary dog." She yawned and took a sip of lemonade. "As for Clarence, *he's* going to balance dishes on a stick between his teeth."

To Baby's delight, Missy dropped the brownie on the ground with a thunk. "Balance dishes? On a stick?"

"Pretty amazing, huh?" Stephanie mimicked Missy.

That was the last straw! Missy had decided then and there that the time was right for drastic measures.

"I have an appointment to see Skip Martin," Missy told the bald man who opened the door.

The man flung the door open and grinned. "Skip Martin's the name, and training animals is my game! Which one of you is Missy and which is Baby?"

Missy laughed as she followed Skip into his studio. "I'm Missy and this is my dog, Baby." The studio was colorfully decorated and filled with hoops, balls, and small trampolines. On a table by the wall was something that resembled a miniature circus. Missy walked over to the table and reached out to touch it.

"Oh, please don't touch!" Skip called to Missy. "The kids just had an intense workout."

"The . . . kids?" Missy asked. She couldn't see anyone on the table.

Skip walked over to her and smiled. "The Tweedle Dee Flea Circus! You *have* heard of them? They perform at all the shopping centers! A real class act!"

Missy peered at the little circus. "Excuse me, Mr. Martin, but I don't see any fleas—"

Without warning Skip blew loudly on a shrill whistle. Missy jumped.

"See?" Skip asked, pointing to a tiny trapeze. The trapeze was actually swinging back and forth. There *was* a flea circus. It was just too tiny to see!

Skip began to sing in an operatic bass voice. "They fly through the air with the greatest of ease! The amazingly talented Tweedle Dee Fleeeeeeas!"

Missy smiled politely, wondering who had trained Skip Martin.

"Now, Missy!" Skip said. "What shall we do with Baby?"

"Teach him to do something incredible in an hour," Missy told him.

"In just one hour?" asked Skip with a worried look.

"We have to be home in time for dinner," explained Missy. Then she left Baby and a bag of chocolate brownies in the hands of Skip Martin. Wishing her dog the very best of luck, Missy left to pay a visit to Emily. The Greens lived just two blocks away from Skip Martin's studio.

As Missy approached Emily's house she could hear two people arguing. Missy soon recognized the voices of Emily and Willie! After Missy had banged on the door ten times, Emily finally opened it.

"What is going on?" asked Missy. "I could hear you all the way down the block!"

"It's Willie!" cried Emily. "She's trying to give Sebastian a bath!"

Missy entered the house, where she saw Willie crawling through Emily's hall on her hands and knees.

"That cat needs a bath desperately!" Willie said. "But he keeps hiding under the furniture, and Emily's no help at all!"

"You know, Emily," Missy said carefully. "A bath might improve his chances of getting adopted."

"But Sebastian is scared of water!" Emily insisted. "You would be too if you went through what he did the other day in the pond!"

For almost an hour Missy tried to help drag Sebastian into the bathtub, but it was impossible. The cat was determined not to take a bath. Finally, for the tenth time, he jumped out of Willie's hands and ran into Emily's room.

"Why don't we just forget it?" Emily pleaded, guarding the bed that Sebastian ran under.

"He needs a bath!" insisted Willie, grabbing a hockey stick from Emily's closet. "This will get him out."

Missy couldn't believe her eyes and ears. "Wilhelmina Wagnalls, drop that hockey stick now!" she shouted. "Emily's right. Forget the bath, at least for the time being."

Willie grumbled and dropped the hockey stick. "Well, then we can forget about ever finding him a home. Sebastian will just land up in the animal shelter with all the other stray cats and dogs."

Missy looked at the clock on Emily's night table.

"Sorry, but I have to leave to pick up Baby," she said.

"Pick him up from where?" asked Willie.

"From the studio of Skip Martin, the animal trainer," Missy said proudly. "He taught the famous Tweedle Dee Fleas and now he's teaching Baby to do tricks for the mascot contest."

"What kind of tricks?" Emily wanted to know.

"Oh, by now Baby will probably know how to jump through a flaming hoop, perform back flips, ride a tricycle . . ."

"Roll over!" Missy cried when she finally got to Skip's studio. "You taught Baby to roll over?"

"Sure," Skip said. "It's a great trick."

"It also happens to be one of the only tricks he already knew how to do!" Missy wailed.

Skip handed Missy the remaining brownies and Baby's leash. "What did you expect in one hour?" he asked with an insulted snort. "Clarence the Wonder Dog?"

After dinner Missy noticed that Baby was scratching like crazy. Missy decided it was probably the lavender hair dye, which was slowly beginning to fade. She looked at her dog and sighed. It was already Thursday night, and Baby was as unprepared as ever for the mascot contest on Saturday. Why couldn't he be like Clarence the Wonder Dog?

Baby went over to Missy and began licking her hand. For the first time ever, Missy pulled her hand away. "Go away, Baby! I'm not in the mood!" Baby looked up at Missy curiously and whined. He hung his head.

"Missy! Telephone!" called her father. "It's Stephanie!"

Missy groaned but took the call.

"Guess what?" asked Stephanie excitedly. "Aunt Constance dropped by with Clarence! Can he come over and play with Baby?"

Missy was tired of resisting Stephanie. "Sure. Bring him over," she said wearily.

Baby was thrilled to meet his television idol. The sheepdog and the Dalmatian got along splendidly as they romped through the Fremont house. Missy's parents were impressed with Clarence too—especially when the Wonder Dog banged out a few notes on the piano.

Mrs. Fremont, who gave piano lessons, had to laugh. "He sounds better than some of my students!"

To Missy's relief, Stephanie and Clarence did not stay very long. And Stephanie brought up the mascot contest *only* ten times in ten minutes! Later that night Missy decided to give Baby a good scrub in the bathtub to cure his itching. She rubbed him dry, and together they went to join Mr. and Mrs. Fremont in front of the television, where they were watching the nightly news report.

"Here's an unusual story," chuckled the anchorwoman. "Skip Martin, a Hills Point animal trainer, has reported the disappearance of his famous Tweedle Dee Flea Circus from his studio today. A reward is being offered for any information leading to the fleas' whereabouts."

Missy stared at the television and then at Baby. No wonder he was scratching—the Tweedle Dee Flea Circus had probably escaped right into Baby's coat!

"A reward?" Mr. Fremont laughed. "For a bunch of fleas?"

Missy heard the water gurgling in the bathtub upstairs.

"I have a feeling," said Missy, "that Skip Martin's reward has just gone down the drain."

CHAPTER

7

———

"Forget it!" shouted Betty to the other waiter at The Big Scoop. "I'm not waiting on that table. You saw what happened the last time those girls were here!"

It was Friday afternoon, one day before the mascot contest and Missy, Willie, Stephanie, and Emily were once again at The Big Scoop. This time Stephanie made sure not to sit across the table from Willie.

"I told you we shouldn't have come here," hissed Stephanie. "They *do* remember us."

"Oh, come on, Stephanie," said Missy, taking a sip of ice water. "You don't expect us to give up ice cream sundaes because of a little accident that happened a week ago?"

"A little accident?" exclaimed Stephanie. "It was a disaster! A catastrophe!"

"Think of it this way, Steph," said Willie. "This will give us all a chance to save our reputations."

The girls began studying the menus.

"The Extra, Extra Eat All About It looks pretty good to me," said Missy, smacking her lips.

"I can't believe Ms. Van Sickel is giving us a quiz on Monday," sighed Emily, her eyes still on the menu.

"Neither can I," said Willie. "She knows the mascot contest is this weekend—who is going to want to memorize all of the American presidents from George Washington up?"

"The only presidents I care to know are the ones on my allowance money," Stephanie said, putting down the menu. She looked at Missy. "Besides, I was planning to celebrate all weekend after Clarence wins the mascot contest."

Missy felt her grip tighten on her menu. She tried to ignore Stephanie.

"I wish there were some kind of trick to memorizing all those presidents without studying," Missy said.

"There is!" Willie said. "All you have to do is read the names of the presidents out loud into a tape recorder, then have someone play it back to you while you sleep!"

"While I sleep?" asked Missy, confused.

"Sure," Willie answered. "When you wake up, you'll know all the presidents by heart. It has something to do with hypnosis. I never tried it, but I saw someone talk about it on a scientific TV show."

"Well, that is the most ridiculous thing I've ever heard in my life!" Stephanie laughed. "Studying in your sleep—"

All of a sudden they heard a loud "Meoowww-www!!"

Stephanie shot Willie an angry look. "Willie Wagnalls, you know how much I hate it when you do that!"

"It wasn't me! Honest!" insisted Willie.

"Meoowwwwww!" There it was again.

Missy, Willie, and Stephanie looked around and under the table. Then Emily spoke up.

"This is where it's coming from," she confessed, picking up her knapsack from under the seat. Her three friends stared in amazement when out peeked Sebastian!

"I have only two more days to keep Sebastian before he goes to the animal shelter," said Emily. "I want to spend as much time with him as possible."

Stephanie snorted with disgust. "I can't figure out why you're so ape over that scruffy, dirty thing!"

"Sebastian is not a thing!" insisted Emily. "He's a tiger cat, and a very smart one too. You should see the things I taught him to do."

"What did you teach him to do, Emily?" asked Missy.

"Well, for one thing—" Emily began to explain but was interrupted by Stephanie.

"Quick!" she said. "Hide that gross thing! Our waiter is coming!"

By now Sebastian's head was completely out of the knapsack. Emily tried gently to push his face back in, but it was no use. He wouldn't budge.

Stephanie groaned impatiently, lifting her water glass. "Get back in, cat!" she ordered, splashing water on Sebastian's face.

"Stephanie, don't!" screamed Emily. "He's afraid of water!"

But it was too late. The sputtering cat let out a scream and frantically clawed himself out of the knapsack.

"Don't let him out!" shouted Missy.

All eyes in The Big Scoop were once again on Missy and her friends.

"Hey! What's going on?" called Paul, their waiter. Just as Paul approached the table, Sebastian tore himself out of the knapsack.

"Get him!" shouted Missy as she, Willie, and Emily chased the cat around the ice cream parlor. Stephanie sank deep into her seat. "I am *so* embarrassed," she moaned.

Sebastian hopped onto a table where a two-year-old boy sat with his mother. "Kitty!" laughed the little boy, pointing to the cat.

Next Sebastian jumped up on the counter, sliding across the smooth, slippery surface.

"Get that cat out of here!" shouted the hefty man behind the counter as Sebastian whizzed by. He held on to a tower of glasses to keep them from toppling over.

Missy ran to the end of the counter to catch Sebastian, but the cat had already made a flying leap for the Tiffany chandelier hanging from the ceiling. The chandelier swung back and forth while the frightened Sebastian clung to it.

Missy, Willie, and Emily formed a circle under

the chandelier and began chanting, "Jump! Jump! Jump!"

Suddenly Betty came out of the kitchen holding a tray of sundaes. "Banana splits coming through!" she called out coldly as Missy, Emily, and Willie reluctantly spread out to let the waitress pass.

"Look out!" screamed Emily. Just as Betty was walking underneath the chandelier, Sebastian jumped off, landing with a clatter onto Betty's tray. The waitress screamed as the banana splits were knocked to the floor with a resounding crash.

Emily grabbed Sebastian just as he began licking the whipped cream off the floor.

Missy, Willie, Stephanie, and Emily made a mad dash for the door.

"I guess that's what they call letting the cat out of the bag!" Missy said as they spilled out of The Big Scoop.

"I will never go back to that place again!" cried Stephanie. "Ever!"

"Hi, Mom, Dad," said Missy as she entered the kitchen. Her parents were busy cutting vegetables for a salad. "Where's Baby?"

"He's asleep in the living room," answered Mrs. Fremont, peeling a carrot. "All that preparation for tomorrow's mascot contest has probably knocked him out."

Asleep? Missy's eyes lit up as she remembered the scientific TV show Willie had mentioned at The Big Scoop. "Mom . . . is Baby . . . *fast* asleep?"

Her father answered as he popped a mushroom into Missy's mouth. "Fast asleep and dreaming of leftovers!"

"Great!" exclaimed Missy. Even if Baby didn't have a chance with beauty or talent, he might still have a chance with the intelligence competition. "Do you think I still have that cassette of alphabet songs you both gave me when I was in kindergarten?" she asked her parents.

"I'm sure you do," answered Mrs. Fremont.

"I thought you knew your ABC's, Missy." Mr. Fremont smiled.

"Oh, Dad!" exclaimed Missy. "It's not for me to listen to. It's for Baby!" She saw the puzzled look on their faces and sighed. "I'll explain later."

In her room Missy rummaged through her closet for her cassette recorder and the alphabet songs. If she played the cassette while Baby slept, would he wake up knowing the alphabet? Of course Baby wouldn't be able to recite the ABC's for Coach Harris and Ms. Van Sickel at the mascot contest, but he might be able to point out certain letters with his paws.

"Why don't I ever label my cassettes?" complained Missy as she tried to find the one containing the alphabet songs. She picked up a cassette from the bottom of the pile. "This is probably it. It's all sticky, so I probably used it back in kindergarten."

Missy tiptoed down to the living room where Baby slept, the cassette recorder under her arm.

"He's still asleep," she thought cheerfully, placing the cassette recorder next to Baby's ear.

Snapping the cassette in, she pushed the button marked Play and waited for the alphabet music to begin. "When he wakes up, he'll be brilliant!" Missy whispered to herself.

After a click and a whirl, the music began to play, but it was not what Missy had expected.

"Oh, no! It's the Blast-Offs!" wailed Missy. The Blast-Offs were a wild and loud rock group. The only reason the cassette was sticky was that Willie had dropped a caramel apple on it at her Halloween party!

The sound of banging drums and twanging guitars made Baby wake up with a start. He let out a frightened howl as he leapt to his feet.

Missy stared helplessly as she watched her dog running around in circles.

"Oh, why don't I just give up, Baby?" she cried angrily. "You'll never be like Clarence the Wonder Dog! You'll never be perfect!"

Perfect. Missy froze when she heard herself say the word. Is that what she expected Baby to be? Perfect?

"Kids who try to be 'perfect' aren't always perfectly happy," her mother had said to her once.

"I wonder if that's also true for sheepdogs," Missy said aloud, staring at Baby. He was hiding behind the sofa and didn't look happy at all. Missy realized that in just one week, Baby had been dyed lavender, rolled over and over, invaded by a flea circus, and jolted out of a deep sleep.

"What am I doing to my best friend?" cried Missy. She shut off the Blast-Offs just as her parents came into the living room.

"Is anything wrong?" asked Mrs. Fremont.

"Oh, Mom, Dad! Baby is miserable and all because I expected him to be the perfect pet for the mascot contest!" Missy told her parents. "Do you think he'll ever forgive me?"

Mr. Fremont put his hand on Missy's shoulder. "I think only Baby can answer that question, honey."

Missy slowly and carefully joined Baby behind the sofa. He was shaking when Missy threw her arms around his neck. Baby looked up at her. After a few seconds he barked softly and began licking her face. Missy laughed with relief—he *did* forgive her!

"Promise me one thing, Baby," she said as she hugged the big sheepdog. "Promise me you'll always stay exactly the way you are!"

CHAPTER

8

The long-awaited day had finally arrived! "Okay, team," Coach Harris said as the Hills Point varsity soccer team met in a huddle during time-out. "The score may be tied, but those Crestview Waves are tough cookies!"

Missy looked over her shoulder at the opposing team. The players were all twice her size. "Those Waves make us look like low tide, Coach Harris."

Coach Harris pretended not to hear Missy's remark as he proceeded to bark out instructions. "Willie, cover that goal. Missy, a little more kicking power. Stephanie, pay attention. Now, all we need is one more point and the game is ours—so let's hustle!"

The coach turned to the bleachers, where the students from Hills Point School sat with their potential mascots. "And you up there!" he shouted. "I want a little more spirit!"

"Yayyyyy, Hills Point!" chanted a few fifth graders.

"Hills Point, Hills Point, squawwwwkkk!" cried a pet parrot.

From where she stood, Missy could see Baby lazily stretched out in front of the bleachers, his head resting on his paws.

Coach Harris gave the thumbs-up signal and the team scurried to their positions on the field.

"I'm worried about Emily," Missy said to Willie. "She never showed up for the game."

"I wish we could call her," said Willie. "But there aren't any phones nearby."

Stephanie looked worried, too, but Missy knew it wasn't about Emily. The game was almost over and Aunt Constance and Clarence the Wonder Dog still hadn't arrived for the mascot contest.

Stephanie took her position next to Ms. Van Sickel. Their teacher was the referee and the one to restart the game. When the ball was dropped, Stephanie snared it, sending it over to the Hills Point team.

The ball was passed from one player to another until it finally landed next to Missy. Missy trapped the ball with her foot and began moving it down field toward the next player. She dribbled the ball lightly and carefully, running into the enemy territory. Keeping her eye on the ball, she took a moment to glance up. "Oh, great," moaned Missy. "Just my luck."

Hilary Stark, the largest Crestview Wave, whom

everyone called The Bulldozer, was closing in on her!

"Grrrrrr!" snarled Hilary as she planted herself in Missy's path.

The second Baby saw The Bulldozer looming over Missy, he picked his head up and growled. In a flash the big sheepdog was running away from the bleachers and onto the soccer field.

"Baby, go back!" shouted Missy as Baby charged toward Hilary.

"What the—?" exclaimed Hilary with surprise as she tried to back away from Baby.

The Hills Point School cheered wildly as they watched Baby clumsily tackle the opposing player. Missy covered her eyes with her hands. "I can't watch," she groaned.

When she finally peeked through her fingers, Missy saw Hilary Stark sprawled on the ground— with Baby sitting on top of her!

"I don't believe this!" The Bulldozer was saying over and over again. "I don't believe this!"

Missy ran over to pry Baby off, but the dog wouldn't move. "It's okay, Baby, she wasn't trying to hurt me—it's all part of the game!"

Baby looked up at Missy. After sniffing at Hilary a couple of times, he let out a low bark and stood up.

Missy went to apologize to Coach Harris and Coach Feldman, the coach for the Crestview Waves. Surprisingly, the two coaches were amused.

"Your dog is quite a soccer player," chuckled Coach Feldman.

The Crestview Waves were also laughing the whole thing off.

"You should have seen your face when you saw that dog, Hilary!" said one Wave. "I wish someone had a video camera!"

"I do too!" Hilary laughed. "Who is ever going to believe it?"

When the excitement finally died down, Ms. Van Sickel blew the whistle to continue the game. The ball was thrown up in the air and again Stephanie kicked it to the Hills Point team. This time it landed directly in front of Missy. Missy looked down at the ball and gritted her teeth. With an extra burst of power she kicked it so low and hard that it sailed past the Crestview goalkeeper and into the net! The bleachers rocked with excitement as the Hills Point spectators cheered, barked, chirped, and croaked. The Hills Point varsity soccer team had won the game!

While the two teams shook hands and said good-by, Hilary Stark walked over to Missy.

"Hey, you're lucky to have a dog like Baby," the Bulldozer said cheerfully, slapping Missy on the back. "My dog Coco is such a wimp."

As the Crestview van pulled out, all eyes were on Ms. Van Sickel. The moment everyone was waiting for had finally arrived!

"Let the mascot contest begin!" Ms. Van Sickel announced.

Missy stood in line with Baby while Ms. Van Sickel and Coach Harris listed the names of all the pets on their clipboards. Missy could see Stephanie nervously pacing back and forth.

"Where's Clarence the Wonder Dog, Stephanie?" asked Willie.

"Oh, I suppose he'll be making a grand entrance," Stephanie answered, trying to appear calm. "He is a star, you know."

After all the pets were neatly recorded, Ms. Van Sickel called out, "The first competition will be for beauty and charm!"

Missy joined the others as they proudly paraded their pets in a circle.

"You look terrific, Baby," she whispered. "Even if you do still have a touch of lavender here and there." Missy had managed to comb out Baby's party streamer tail the night before.

"The next competition will be for talent!" announced Coach Harris. Missy ran to get a double-fudge brownie from her bag. Baby performed his famous roll-over trick, his eyes never leaving the brownie over his head.

But everyone's favorite was Icky the garden snake, who formed the shape of a heart while Candice Kramer played a love song on the recorder.

"That's disgusting!" whispered Stephanie to Missy and Willie.

"They don't think so," Missy said, nodding toward the bleachers. Candice Kramer had five brothers and sisters who were all cheering and holding up signs that read "Icky for Mascot," and "Slither to Victory, Icky!"

"The next competition will be for intelligence," Ms. Van Sickel announced.

Harvey's pet robot began reciting what Harvey explained was the Pledge of Allegiance.

"That doesn't sound like the Pledge of Allegiance to me, Harvey," said Ms. Van Sickel.

"It is," insisted Harvey. "But when I finally programmed it . . . it came out backward!"

"How do you know it's the Pledge of Allegiance?" snapped Stephanie to the others. "For all we know, it's his grocery list!"

When all eyes were finally on Baby, Missy decided to take a chance. "Baby, how much is one and one?" To her surprise, Baby barked two times! "Wow!" said Missy to herself. "He's smarter than I thought."

"And now for the final competition!" Coach Harris shouted. "School spirit!"

Missy walked over to Ms. Van Sickel and Coach Harris. "Should Baby and I sit this one out?" she asked. "We have nothing prepared for the school spirit competition."

"Why, Melissa Fremont!" cried Ms. Van Sickel. "Baby proved his school spirit when he tackled the opposing player during the game. We already gave him ten points!"

Missy felt her face glowing. She couldn't remember a day when she felt happier. Baby's chances were better than ever now. He had come through the whole mascot contest with flying colors, and best of all, he did it by being himself!

After the rest of the pets proved their school

spirit, the time had finally come for Ms. Van Sickel and Coach Harris to choose the mascot.

"But you can't pick the mascot!" Stephanie began to wail. "My contestant hasn't arrived yet!"

"But, Stephanie," said Coach Harris, "there's just no telling how long we might have to wait."

"You have to wait!" Stephanie whined. "My contestant is special!"

"All of these pets are special, Stephanie," Ms. Van Sickel said firmly.

All of a sudden Willie cried out, "Look, here comes Emily!"

Everyone turned to see Emily Green in the distance, running toward the field.

"That's Emily all right," said Missy. "But what's in that huge basket she's carrying?"

CHAPTER

9

"I'm sorry I missed the game," said Emily breathlessly. She placed the basket on the ground with a thud.

"Can you tell us what's in the basket, Em?" asked Missy.

"From the size of it, I imagine it's Emily's lunch," sneered Stephanie. Willie gave Stephanie a jab with her elbow.

Emily bent down to open the latch and lift the lid. From the basket she carefully pulled out the most beautiful cat. It was cream-colored with shiny black stripes. Its fur was soft and fluffy and around its neck was a baby-blue satin ribbon.

"Why, what a handsome cat!" said Coach Harris.

"I didn't know you had a pet, Emily," Ms. Van Sickel said. "What's his name?"

"Sebastian!" announced Emily proudly.

"That's . . . Sebastian?" gasped Missy in amazement.

"I thought Sebastian was afraid of water, Emily," said Willie. "How did you get him so clean?"

"I read in a magazine that Queen Cleopatra used to take baths in milk," explained Emily. "So I gave Sebastian a milk bath and he loved it!"

With Sebastian in her arms, Emily walked over to Coach Harris and Ms. Van Sickel. "I know I'm late," she said. "But I'd still like to enter Sebastian in the mascot contest."

"How can she?" whispered Missy to Willie. "Sebastian has to go to the animal shelter tomorrow morning!"

"I don't know!" answered Willie with surprise.

Stephanie stomped over to the judges. "Ms. Van Sickel! Coach Harris! Under all that ribbon and fluff is a pathetic alley cat. Besides, you said yourself that it's too late to enter!"

"Well." Ms. Van Sickel thought out loud. "He is here now . . . and we didn't choose the mascot yet."

"I know," said Coach Harris. "Why not let the Hills Point School decide?"

A quick show of hands made the decision— Sebastian would compete! Even Icky the garden snake's campaigners wanted to see what the cat could do.

"Okay, Emily." Coach Harris smiled. "Let Sebastian do his stuff."

Emily nodded and cleared her throat. "Ladies and gentlemen and children of all ages!" she shouted.

"Oh, brother!" groaned Stephanie, rolling her eyes.

"For the talent competition," Emily continued, "Sebastian will jump through a hoop before your very eyes!" Emily formed a hoop with her arms. Everyone clapped as Sebastian jumped in and out of it three times!

"For the intelligence competition, Sebastian will demonstrate an amazing ability to recognize lunch!" announced Emily, pulling from the basket a small red bowl, a can of tuna fish, and a can opener. All of Hills Point School went wild as Sebastian pushed his bowl along the ground to the whishing sound of the can opener.

"And last but not least," Emily declared, "Sebastian will astound and amaze you with his school spirit!" She pulled out a miniature pompom in the school colors and placed it between Sebastian's teeth. The cat immediately began swinging it back and forth—cheerleader style!

By now everyone was chanting, "We want Sebastian! Yayyyy, Sebastian!" Even those with pets of their own had to agree that the striped cat was pretty amazing.

"So that's what Emily was teaching Sebastian to do!" Missy smiled at her friend.

Candice Kramer's brothers and sisters were already throwing down their signs.

"I told you we should have Icky spell out 'Hills Point School' with his body!" Candice's brother complained.

While Ms. Van Sickel and Coach Harris studied the scores, Missy put her arm around Baby.

"It's still a close contest," she thought. "Baby still has a good chance."

After a few minutes the judges returned and announced their decision.

"The mascot for the Hills Point varsity soccer team will be . . . Sebastian the cat!" Coach Harris shouted.

Missy closed her eyes and rested her cheek on Baby's furry head. "You did great, Baby," she whispered. "Thanks for trying."

As she hugged Baby, Emily came running over.

"Missy, what will I do?" Emily cried. "Sebastian can't be our mascot. He still has to go to the animal shelter tomorrow."

"That's what I thought," said Missy. "Why did you enter him in the contest then, Emily?"

"I did it to show everyone, including Stephanie, what a great cat Sebastian really is," explained Emily.

Missy put her hand on Emily's arm. "I would have done the same thing, Em."

"What will I tell Coach Harris and Ms. Van Sickel?" moaned Emily.

"I think the best thing is to tell them the truth," Missy said softly.

Missy and Willie stood next to Emily as she explained her sticky situation.

"You know, Emily," said Ms. Van Sickel gently. "Entering Sebastian in the contest when you knew he had to be given away wasn't fair to your classmates *or* to Sebastian."

Blinking back tears, Emily nodded.

"But how's this for an idea, Emily?" Ms. Van Sickel asked after thinking for a while. "We can set up a little home for Sebastian in the gym. He'll have a place to live and everyone on the team can take turns caring for him in between games."

"*And* he wouldn't have to go to the animal shelter," added Coach Harris.

Missy, Willie, and Emily shrieked happily and began jumping up and down.

"Isn't that wonderful?" cried Emily. "I am *sooooo* happy!"

Seeing the radiant look on Emily Green's face, Missy decided that if Baby was going to lose the mascot contest, she was glad it was to Sebastian.

"Hills Point Alley Cats," muttered Stephanie angrily. "Give me a break!"

Suddenly they were interrupted by a commotion coming from the other side of the soccer field. Aunt Constance had just arrived—with Professor Pesty, who was wearing a pair of fake dog ears and a tail!

"Woof! Woof!" he barked as he crawled around on his hands and knees. "Where do I sign up for the mascot contest? Woof! Woof!"

Professor Pesty needed no introduction. Almost everyone recognized the hilarious television star.

"Now you'll see what a real mascot is made of," Stephanie told the eager fans as she burst through, trying to get to Aunt Constance.

"Aunt Constance," she asked her aunt. "Where's Clarence? He is still coming, isn't he? Isn't he?"

"Oh, Stephanie," Aunt Constance sighed. "I hate to tell you this, but Clarence won't be coming today."

"Won't be coming?" Stephanie repeated. "But he has to!"

"I wish he could, but Clarence has come down with the most unusual case of . . . of fleas," said Aunt Constance.

"Fleas?" gawked Stephanie. "Well, so what? Throw him in the bathtub!"

"I wish it were that easy, Stephanie," said Aunt Constance. "But Clarence is allergic to fleas, so he'll be needing extra special care around the clock."

"How did he get fleas anyway?" demanded Stephanie.

Aunt Constance raised her shoulders. "Who knows?"

But Missy knew. Clarence most probably had picked up a few Tweedle Dee Fleas when he came to visit Baby! If the fleas could jump from one tiny trapeze to another, they could certainly jump from Baby to Clarence.

Missy muffled a giggle as she watched Stephanie looking like one of Harvey's robots—about to blow a circuit.

"Not only did Clarence miss your mascot contest," continued Aunt Constance. "But he'll have to miss two shows next week."

Professor Pesty began swinging his fake tail. "I'd fill in for him myself," he joked. "But my nose just isn't cold enough!"

Missy joined everyone as they howled over Professor Pesty's zany antics.

"What we need now is another animal to fill in for Clarence until he recovers," Aunt Constance said, rubbing her chin.

"How about a snake?" asked Candice Kramer, holding Icky in front of Aunt Constance.

Aunt Constance looked doubtful. "A snake isn't exactly what I . . . had in mind."

"I know," cried Professor Pesty. "How about that sheepdog?" He pointed at Baby.

Missy, Willie, and Emily looked at one another excitedly. "Baby!" they all said in unison.

"Well, I hear he has talent," Aunt Constance said, smiling.

Stephanie looked horrified. "Aunt Constance, Mr. Pesty—if you put that dog on your show, you'll be making a big mistake! He's nothing but a—a ham!"

"Just what we need," Professor Pesty declared.

Missy let out a whoop. "Baby, you're going to be a star after all!" she cried.

"Oh, great." Stephanie folded her arms in disgust. "Now we've got a scrub mop for a star as well as an alley cat for a mascot."

"Wait a minute!" Missy said. "Where is Sebastian anyway?"

Everyone looked around to see where Sebastian had gone.

"There he is!" shouted Harvey. "He's in the bleachers sleeping on someone's sweat shirt!"

Stephanie snarled as she ran toward the bleachers. "That sweat shirt happens to be mine!"

"Uh-oh," said Willie to Missy and Emily. "There's no telling what Stephanie will do to that cat now. We'd better go after her."

Emily began biting her nails. "I hope she doesn't hurt Sebastian!"

"Come on, Baby!" Missy called. "You might have to tackle Stephanie now!"

By the time they reached the bleachers, Stephanie was standing over the sleeping cat. Missy could see that she was watching Sebastian's body heave up and down as he lay curled up in a little striped ball. Stephanie seemed to be slightly fascinated as she stared at Sebastian for the longest time. Finally she spoke.

"Sebastian is lying on my designer sweat shirt," she said. "Which can mean only one thing."

"What?" demanded Missy, preparing to hold Stephanie back.

Stephanie's face softened. "It means . . . that this cat has *extremely* good taste!"

Then, to everyone's surprise, Ms. Perfect knelt down to pet Sebastian.

"The Hills Point Tiger Cats," she cooed. "I kind of like that."

"Yeah." Willie remarked. "And a cat is better than a boy in a chicken suit any day!"

Missy leaned on Baby and breathed a sigh of relief.

"Girls, shake a leg!" Coach Harris called cheerfully from the soccer field. "Professor Pesty wants to take the whole team out for a victory celebration!"

"Yes," added Ms. Van Sickel. "At The Big Scoop!"

Missy, Willie, Emily, and Stephanie looked at one another the second they heard the name of the ice cream parlor.

"The Big . . . Scoop?" they gulped.

Slowly they began to giggle until soon they were rolling on the ground, shaking with laughter.

"I think we'd better tell Professor Pesty," said Missy, wiping a tear from her eye, "that from now on we celebrate all our victories . . . at Pizza Paradise!"